"Jack... Bed time!"

"Awww, but I don't want to go to bed," Jack complained, "Sometimes I get scared at night."

"What's there to be scared of buddy?" Papa asked.

Jack thought for a second.
"Well, I'm scared of the dark, I'm scared of snakes and spiders, I'm scared of thunder, I'm scared of the dentist. But most of all, I'm scared of satan and demons."

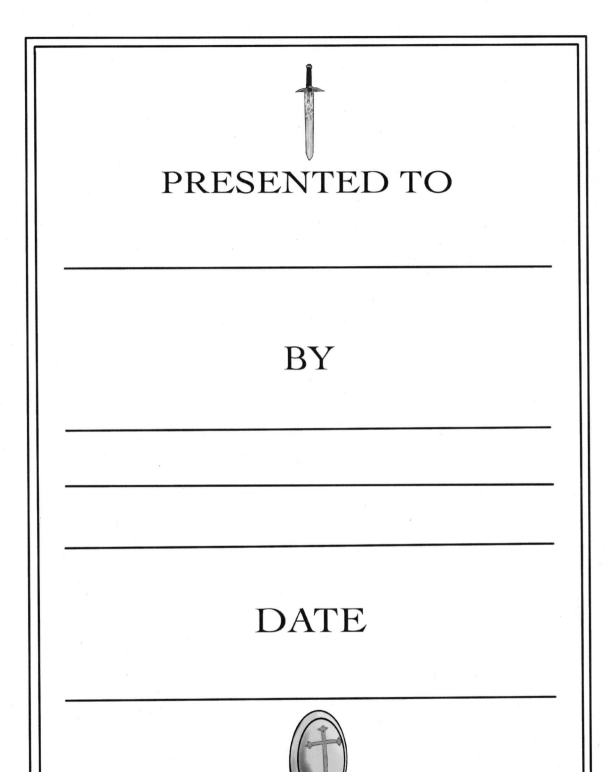

PRESENTED TO

_____

BY

_____

_____

_____

DATE

_____

The Armor of God

A Children's Book
Exploring the Holy
Scriptures of Ephesians 6

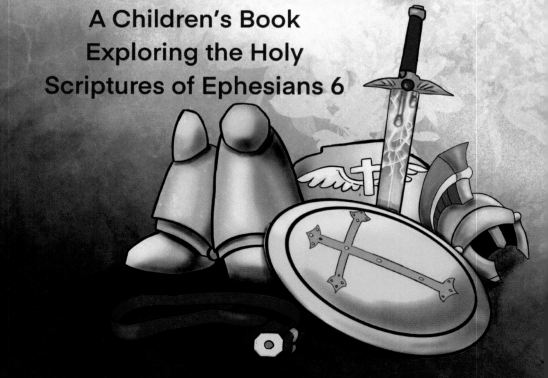

Papa sat and rested his hand on Jack's shoulder. "Well, I can't help you with the dentist, he scares me too." Papa said with a chuckle. "But you don't need to be afraid of those other things, especially satan and his goofy little demons. Don't you know that when you are a soldier in God's army, satan and demons are actually scared of you?!"

"Really!" Shouted Jack. "How do I become a soldier in God's army?"

"Hahaha," Papa laughed with a smile. "You already are a soldier in God's army. You already know Jesus in your heart and asked Him to be your savior right?

Confused, Jack answered. "Well... yes I did."

Papa squeezed Jack's shoulder a little tighter and said,
"Then your sins are forgiven. You are no longer an enemy of
God and you are now adopted into His family. Therefore, you are
a member of His army. But I do see how such a strong warrior
like yourself might feel a little vulnerable without his armor."

"My armor?" Asked Jack.

"Let's get out the Bible," said Papa, "and I'll show you how
to get armored up. What do you say!"

"Yes!" Jack shouted with a loud and bold voice.
"Let's do it!"

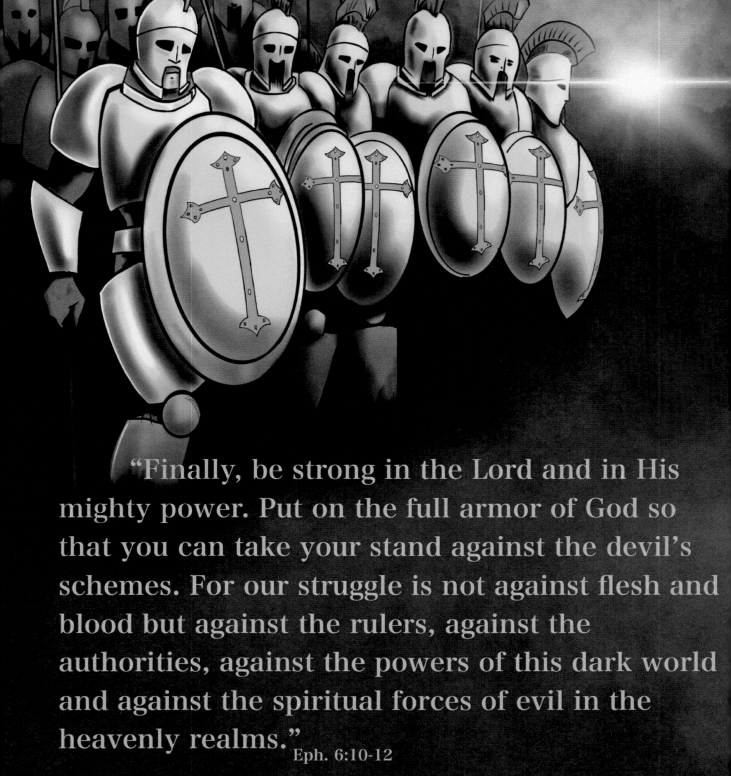

"Finally, be strong in the Lord and in His mighty power. Put on the full armor of God so that you can take your stand against the devil's schemes. For our struggle is not against flesh and blood but against the rulers, against the authorities, against the powers of this dark world and against the spiritual forces of evil in the heavenly realms."

Eph. 6:10-12

"Therefore put on the full armor of God so that when the day of evil comes, you may be able to stand your ground." Eph. 6:13

"And after you have done everything to stand, stand firm with the belt of truth buckled around your waist." Eph 6:14

The belt of truth is the truth of God and
the truth of His Word. We wrap it around us
and it holds everything together.

"Put on the breast plate of righteousness."

Eph 6:14

The breastplate of righteousness covers and protects our hearts. When we trust in Jesus, God sees righteousness in the perfection of Jesus Christ.

"Get your feet fitted with the readiness that comes from the gospel of peace."

Eph 6:15

This gives us the opportunity to run and tell everyone about the good news of Jesus Christ. And we can bring peace by changing the hearts and minds of our enemies.

When the devil tries to hurt us by telling us lies, we can hold up the shield, which is our faith in Christ, and we can block those lies and extingush the devil's fiery darts.

"And take the helmet of salvation," Eph 6:17

The helmet guards our thoughts and our minds and reminds us that we are saved by Jesus Christ.

"And take the Sword of the Spirit, which is the Word of God;"
Eph 6:17

Not only does God give us armor to protect ourselves, but he also gives us a weapon to fight back. The Sword of the Spirit is the Holy Word of God.

When you hold the Word of God then you hold the truth of God's Word. This is the most powerful weapon in the world and you should never leave home without it.

"I'm not scared anymore!" Jack shouted.

Jack, you are a mighty man of Christ, and a fearless soldier in God's army. The Bible says "Be strong and of good courage, do not fear nor be afraid for the Lord your God is with you; He will not leave you nor foresake you." I pray you have the faith of Abraham, the courage of Joshua, the wisdom of Solomon, the strength of Sampson, and the heart of the Lion of the Tribe of Judah, who is our Lord Jesus Christ. May you walk faithfully with the Lord for all of your days.

Sweet dreams. God bless you.
I love you.

THE
END

Mission and Message

Proverbs 18:21.

"Death and life are in the power of the toungue, and those who love it will eat its fruits."

Romans 10:17

"So faith comes from hearing, and hearing through the word of Christ."

Words are incredibly powerful. As parents, we can use our words to pour into our children, speak life and blessings over them. We can build them up with knowledge , confidence and faith. Christian parents should always be looking for opportunities to speak truth into our children. What better of an opportunity then at night when it's time for that bedtime story? That rare moment in the day when we have our child's undivided attention.

When The Lord chose to bless me with children, one of my favorite and most charrished moments was to read to them. My mission was to take advantage of reading time and find books that spoke Biblical truths with Biblical lessons. Most importantly, books that quote scripture, word for word that wouldn't necessarily bore them to sleep. I never could quite find what I was looking for so I decided to write and illustrate it with my son.

I pray this book is a blessing to you and your child!

Made in the USA
Monee, IL
15 February 2023